CHARMING CHRISTMAS

KAY CORRELL

ZURA LU PUBLISHING LLC

Published by Zura Lu Publishing LLC

101520

This book is dedicated to those delightful, happy-ending Christmas movies I so love to watch.

KAY'S BOOKS

Find more information on all my books at
kaycorrell.com

COMFORT CROSSING ~ THE SERIES

The Shop on Main - Book One
The Memory Box - Book Two
The Christmas Cottage - A Holiday Novella
(Book 2.5)
The Letter - Book Three
The Christmas Scarf - A Holiday Novella
(Book 3.5)
The Magnolia Cafe - Book Four
The Unexpected Wedding - Book Five

The Wedding in the Grove - (a crossover short

story between series - with Josephine and Paul from The Letter.)

LIGHTHOUSE POINT ~ THE SERIES
Wish Upon a Shell - Book One
Wedding on the Beach - Book Two
Love at the Lighthouse - Book Three
Cottage near the Point - Book Four
Return to the Island - Book Five
Bungalow by the Bay - Book Six

CHARMING INN ~ Return to Lighthouse Point
One Simple Wish - Book One
Two of a Kind - Book Two
Three Little Things - Book Three
Four Short Weeks - Book Four
Five Years or So - Book Five
Six Hours Away - Book Six
Charming Christmas - Book Seven

SWEET RIVER ~ THE SERIES
A Dream to Believe in - Book One
A Memory to Cherish - Book Two
A Song to Remember - Book Three
A Time to Forgive - Book Four

A Summer of Secrets - Book Five
A Moment in the Moonlight - Book Six

MOONBEAM BAY - coming 2021
The Parker Women
The Parker Cafe
A Heather Parker Original
The Parker Family Secret
Grace Parker's Peach Pie

INDIGO BAY ~ A multi-author sweet romance series

Sweet Days by the Bay - Kay's Complete Collection of stories in the Indigo Bay series

Or buy them separately:

Sweet Sunrise - Book Three
Sweet Holiday Memories - A short holiday story
Sweet Starlight - Book Nine

Sign up for my newsletter at my website *kaycorrell.com* to make sure you don't miss any new releases or sales.

CHAPTER 1

C harlotte Duncan wanted everything to be perfect for her wedding. Really, what woman doesn't? But she really, *really* wanted it perfect. Seriously perfect.

She had so many dreams about what her wedding would be like. What she'd wear. The decorations. The music. The cake.

But right now she had a big problem with the whole perfect wedding thing...

She had no place to get married, and the wedding was just weeks away.

She and Ben had decided to get married at Charming Inn, but a new girl working at the inn had double-booked another wedding on their date. And she'd taken a large deposit for the other wedding.

Lillian, as owner of Charming Inn, had offered the inn to Charlotte free of charge. But of course, she didn't want Lillian to give up income. There was also the not-so-tiny detail that the invitations had already gone out... listing Charming Inn as the venue.

Charlotte walked down Oak Street, ignoring the cheerful Christmas decorations on the storefronts and the lines of Christmas lights and wreaths strung across the street. Why had she chosen Christmastime to get married? Everyone was wanting venues to throw holiday parties. How in the world would she find a place to hold the wedding at this late date?

She slipped into The Lucky Duck—wishing some of the luck would rub off on her—and waved to Willie, the owner, as she slid into a booth to wait for her best friends, Sara and Robin.

Best friends who had both recently gotten married and pulled off their weddings without a hitch. Obviously they had more luck going for them than she did.

Cheerful holiday music spilled around her. Good try. It did nothing to improve her mood.

She sat and stared off into space until Robin slid into the seat across from her, followed closely by Sara.

"Don't worry, Charlotte. We're going to figure this all out." Robin reached across and squeezed her hand.

"Right. Within two weeks we need to find another place for the wedding, and who knows what else will go wrong between now and then." She was normally a look-on-the-bright-side person, but not since hearing the news that she'd lost her venue.

"You could take Aunt Lillian up on her offer to still hold your wedding instead of the duplicate. You did schedule first." Sara pulled a notebook out of her purse.

"No, I'm not going to take a paying event away from Lillian and I'm not going to disappoint that bride either. It's not her fault."

Robin sighed. "It's my fault for letting the new girl handle some event scheduling. That won't happen again. And she feels terrible if that's any consolation."

"I'm sure it was an honest mistake." Charlotte frowned. But a messy one nonetheless.

"Why she thought that there would be an

open slot on a weekend so close to Christmas is beyond me." Robin scowled, leaning back against the worn wooden back of the booth. "This is such a mess."

"No, it's not, because we're going to fix it." Sara grabbed a pen.

Willie came over to their table. "You three look serious."

"There's been a mess up with scheduling at Charming Inn for Charlotte's wedding. We need to find a new place," Sara explained.

"I don't know how we'll find a place so last minute." She turned to Willie. "I'll have one of your magical basil motonics. I hear they cure everything."

Willie grinned. "They do. So I'm told."

"I'll have one, too," Sara chimed in.

"Me, too. Don't want them to drink alone," Robin added. "And how about an order of hushpuppies and... oh, a slice of chocolate cake with three forks. We need our comfort food."

Willie laughed. "Coming right up."

"Okay, so any idea on where we could move the wedding?" Sara's forehead creased as she tapped her pen on the table. "We should be able to come up with somewhere."

"I don't want it to just be somewhere. I want it to be... special. Like having it at Charming Inn would be special." She wadded up the napkin in front of her, debating lobbing it across the room in frustration.

"The community center?" Robin suggested.

"I already checked with Noah." Sara shook her head. "It's booked for a Christmas party."

"We need to come up with some kind of creative idea or I'm going to hear no end of I-told-you-sos from my mother and sister. They told me I wasn't leaving enough time to plan the wedding."

"But you did... everything was perfect." Sara pursed her lips.

"Until it wasn't." She hated to hear the poor-me tone in her voice... but to be honest... poor me fit the situation right now.

"Okay, we'll have to keep brainstorming places." Robin smiled encouragingly. "And you shouldn't ever listen to your sister, anyway."

Willie brought over their drinks and food. Charlotte sipped her drink and downed too many hushpuppies as idea after idea for a venue got shot down. Robin made phone calls for each new place they came up with, but no one had availability.

Maybe she *would* have to postpone the wedding. Ben wouldn't be happy but her family would. They hadn't been pleased she was having it the weekend she'd chosen anyway. They had fancy Christmas parties they would miss back in Austin, and her mother had the fancy Snow Gala the weekend after her wedding and constantly complained it was going to be so difficult to get away the weekend before the big gala.

"Listen, I'll make some calls when I get back to the inn. I'm sure we can find a place that will be great," Robin said as she took the last bite of the chocolate cake.

Sara's phone beeped and she glanced at it. "Oh, I have to go. I'm supposed to meet Noah for dinner." She laughed. "Not that I'll be hungry after all this, but comfort food was needed."

Robin grabbed the bill. "I've got this." She rose and hugged Charlotte. "Don't worry. I swear we'll come up with the best plan ever."

Her friends left and she sat and sipped on her drink. She should probably go find Ben and tell him they might have to postpone.

Her phone beeped and she saw it was a call from the bridal boutique. Ah, at least that detail

6

was perfect. The dress she'd found was so wonderful. It looked like it had been designed for her with her style in mind. They were probably calling to schedule her last fitting.

She'd originally thought she might have Ruby, Ben's mother, make her wedding dress, but then she'd found the perfect dress at the Bridal Boutique in Sarasota. Plus, she knew Ruby was busy with her own things getting ready for her son's wedding.

"Charlotte, this is Marguerite from the Bridal Boutique."

"Hey, Marguerite. Calling to set up my last fitting?" If she could find a venue so she could have the wedding...

"Ah... about that."

Her heart tumbled in her chest at the somber tone in the normally bubbly owner's voice.

"What?"

"There's been a... mishap. My seamstress took your gown home to work on some of the lace adjustments. And..."

Charlotte closed her eyes, willing the woman to talk faster. Or maybe to stop talking.

"And, unfortunately, her apartment burned."

"Oh, no." Charlotte's eyes flew open. "Is she

okay?"

"Yes, she got out along with her pup. But the dress is damaged beyond repair. I tried to put in a rush order to replace it, but there's just not enough time."

Charlotte slumped back against the seat. Her perfect dress was gone now, too?

"I'm so very sorry," Marguerite said. "Would you want to come in and look for another one? I'll do everything possible to help you find a dress. I just feel awful."

"I... ah... I don't know." She stared at the empty glass, debating ordering another one.

"Why don't you think on it? Call me first thing in the morning. I'm sure we can find something you'll love." Marguerite said the words with forced positivity and encouragement.

Charlotte wasn't buying it. What were the chances of finding another dress she loved that much and it being in her size or close enough to be tailored to fit her? She felt like she looked at a bazillion dresses before she found this one. The one that was now ashes.

"Sure, I'll call tomorrow." Though she was pretty sure that was a lie.

The wedding was conspiring against her.

Maybe her mother and her sister would get their wish, and the wedding would be moved to a new date, one more convenient for them. Never mind it meant postponing getting married to Ben.

Only... she didn't *want* to wait to marry Ben.

But she was a practical woman. A person couldn't get married without a venue or a dress, could they?

She got up and thanked Willie.

"I'm sure you'll find a perfect place for your wedding," Willie said with a smile of encouragement.

Except they'd tried everywhere that they could think of. And even if she did find a place —and it was looking doubtful—she wouldn't have a dress. But she didn't share that depressing fact with Willie. She just gave him a sad smile and headed outside.

She should go talk to Ben, but she wasn't really ready to say it was over. To call it quits. To admit they had too many complications to pull off the wedding as planned.

She decided to take a walk out to Lighthouse Point to clear her head. Nothing like a beach walk to make the world look more hopeful.

And she sure could use some hope about now.

CHAPTER 2

Charlotte stood at Lighthouse Point watching the beautiful sunset out over the gulf. The colors swirled and preened like a peacock on full display but did little to lift her spirits. The breeze tugged at her hair and she caught it back away from her face as she sank down on the cool sand. The waves rolled slowly onto shore. It should soothe her. It should. But even the magic of the waves did little to cheer her out of her self-pitying mood.

Maybe she'd allow herself just a tiny bit of time to wallow in her mood. Then she'd get over it.

Probably.

Possibly. Could a person really get over a ruined wedding?

Well, right there was some good wallowing.

She scooped up a handful of sand and stared at it as it sifted back through her fingers in a slow, comforting flow of grains. A small shell caught her attention. It was nothing special, just a shell with orange streaks on it, and as she turned it over she saw delicate shades of pink.

It was kind of pretty. She normally wasn't much of a shelling person, but this one called to her.

Then, feeling a little silly, she rose from the sand and brushed off her clothes, the shell clutched in her fist. Might as well take advantage of the Lighthouse Point legend... Not that she truly believed in it, of course.

She closed her eyes and made her wish. Then with one more quick look at the shell, she tossed it out into the waves. Just three simple words. Her wish.

Make everything perfect.

There, she'd just see if there was really anything to this legend about wishes made at Lighthouse Point coming true.

She wouldn't say anything to Ben this

evening. She'd let Robin make a few more phone calls. Maybe something would come up.

Maybe she'd find a venue.

Maybe her luck would change.

Of course, there was now the whole issue of a wedding dress...

She took one last look at where the shell had landed in the water and turned to head back to her cottage. Tomorrow had to be a better day, right?

CHAPTER 3

The next morning, Charlotte looked down at her phone sitting on the counter, pinging with text messages from Robin.

Can you meet me at The Sweet Shoppe?

Did you get my text?

Char, answer me.

She texted back to Robin that she could meet her there in ten minutes. She headed out, glad Robin had chosen the bakery to meet because she'd skipped breakfast and a cinnamon roll from Julie's shop was exactly what she needed. And more coffee. She might just eat her way through the weeks until her wedding. You know, since she didn't have a dress to fit into—and if she even got to have her wedding.

Yep, the self-pitying mood was still strangling her. She was developing this wallowing to a fine art.

Anyway, meeting Robin would give her a chance to tell her friend about her other *tiny* problem... the lack of a wedding dress.

She hurried to The Sweet Shoppe and pushed inside. Robin jumped up and motioned her over.

"I got you a cinnamon roll and coffee. Hope that's okay."

"Perfect. Just what I wanted." She settled into the seat across from Robin, reached for the roll, and took a sip of the coffee.

"So, I've got good news." Robin practically bounced in her seat.

"You found a place?"

"Not just a place. You're going to get married at Charming Inn."

"No, I already told you. We're not bumping out that poor bride." She took another sip of coffee. How many times did she have to insist that none of this was the other bride's fault?

"We're not." A self-satisfied grin settled on Robin's face.

She leaned back and stared. "Okay, spill it. What are you talking about?"

"So I ran into Tally last night and told her about our problem. Strangely, she'd just had a cancellation at Magic Cafe. And guess what day that cancellation was for? Yes. Your wedding date. So Magic Cafe is available on your date."

"Really? But you said—"

Robin held up a hand. "So I called the other bride, explained the situation, sent her links to Magic Cafe and she said she loved it. Her wedding is more casual since it's so last minute and she's just sending out e-vites to her close friends. So she'll email them with the change of venue."

"Really?" She sat back, stunned. "So, I'm back on for a wedding at Charming Inn?"

"You are."

"That is great news. Fabulous news." A tentative smile spread across her face.

Julie came over with a pot of coffee. "What's great news? And do you two want refills?"

She nodded and shoved her coffee cup closer to Julie. "There was a mix-up on my wedding at Charming Inn, but Robin has it all sorted out."

"Well, at least we're still good to go on your wedding cake. I can't wait to make it. The design you picked out is lovely."

It *was* a lovely design and Julie made the best cakes ever.

"So, the venue and cake are good now, but I still have a problem." She let out a sigh, wondering why her wedding was fighting her.

"What's that?" Julie asked as she poured more coffee for Robin.

"My wedding dress. It was destroyed in a fire."

"It was?" Robin's eyes flew open wide. "No."

"Yes, I found out last night after you and Sara left The Lucky Duck. And there isn't enough time to get it ordered in again before the wedding."

Julie snapped her fingers. "How about asking Ruby to make you one? She did a wonderful job with Lillian's dress, didn't you think?"

"I had talked to her awhile back and she actually made some sketches. Then I found this dress in the bridal shop and loved it. I figured Ruby would be so busy with the wedding, that buying the dress was smarter and easier on Ruby. Though, I wonder if she could make me one in time." Her forehead creased as she thought about the suggestion. "No, she's busy with the wedding, too. After all, it is her son I'm marrying. I couldn't ask her. And we'd have to order in material and lace and... it's just so soon."

"I have another idea." Julie's laughter spilled around them. "I'm full of them today."

"I'll take all the help I can get."

"I wore the most beautiful dress to my wedding. It was a vintage wedding dress and it has a lot of history. There was a letter in a hidden pocket of the dress from Barbara, the first woman to wear it."

"Really?"

"Anyway, I still have the dress. I bet Barbara would be thrilled if you used it for the basis of a dress for your wedding. The lace is beautiful. A bit of it is torn from over the years, but I'm sure Ruby could work around that."

Robin already had her phone out and was talking to Ruby. She nodded with a big smile on her face and hung up the phone. "Ruby says, of course, she will. And yes, she has time. She's already finished making the dress she's wearing. She said to come over when we're finished here. And Julie, she wondered if you could text her a photo of you in the dress?"

"Of course." Julie dug out her phone and

scrolled through photos. "Here, I found a couple. I'll send them to her."

"Thanks. Ruby said she'd look at the photo and pull out some designs that she thinks you might like, but she said she's open to anything."

"You can get the dress from my house and take it with you."

"Julie, are you sure?" The tiniest bit of hope blossomed in Charlotte's chest.

"I'm sure. That dress has brought a lot of happiness to a lot of marriages. Might as well continue its magic. Barbara would love that."

Julie went to wait on other customers and Charlotte turned to Robin. "So you know how people go out to Lighthouse Point and make a wish?"

"Sure. And remember, you, me, and Sara did when we were young girls."

Charlotte almost blushed, reluctant to admit this to her friend because it sounded kind of... silly... to say it out loud, but she blurted it out. "Because I'm beginning to think there's something to be said for our town's favorite legend of wishes made at Lighthouse Point coming true."

"Never doubted it," Robin said as she nodded.

CHARLOTTE AND ROBIN arrived at Ruby's and were greeted by Mischief and May, Ruby's dogs. The dogs wagged their tails, and Charlotte handed the dress to Robin and bent down to pet them.

She and Robin went and sat at Ruby's dining table, looking over sketches Ruby had made before and leafing through the many fashion illustrations Ruby had collected over the years.

"I'm just not sure what I want." She looked at the papers spread around them, overwhelmed.

"Why don't you slip on Julie's dress and we'll go from there?" Ruby suggested.

Charlotte took the dress into a guest bedroom and put it on. She looked in the mirror and turned this way and that. It really was pretty, if not her style. She ran her hands along the sides to smooth the dress and felt something rustling. She reached into the folds and found the pocket Julie had mentioned. Handling it carefully, she opened the letter and read the note written in swirling script.

I DON'T KNOW who will end up with this wedding dress of mine. I was married to the love of my life in December 1950. We were married for sixty-two years before he passed away. I'm moving to a nursing home now and must part with my beloved dress. I hope it finds just the right person and I pray that whoever ends up with this dress finds as much happiness as I did.

I wish you a beautiful wedding and years of love.
With much love and blessings for your life together,
Barbara

TEARS FLOODED her eyes and she dashed her hand against them, wiping them away. She could just feel the warm wishes of this Barbara from so many years ago. She looked in the mirror again. Yes, this was going to work. She could feel it.

She headed out to show Ruby and Robin.

"Hold out your arm," Ruby commanded. "Turn left. Okay, now turn right."

"It doesn't really look like you, Charlotte. You have this... style about you." Robin shook her head.

The dogs stared at her, tipping their heads this way and that as she turned around.

"But I want this dress. Look at this note." She passed it over for Ruby and Robin to read.

Ruby stood back and rubbed her chin, her lips pursed. "So... I have an idea..."

She sat down, grabbed a pencil and tablet, and started to sketch. Charlotte's eyes grew wide. "You can make that from this?"

"I can. We'll take out that fitted waist and make the dress flow from a higher line, under your bust. Then... we'll take off the arms and I'll make a straight fitted strapless top, like this." Ruby drew some more lines. "I think we have enough lace to make it all about knee length."

"That will be perfect because—" Robin stopped short.

Charlotte cocked her head and narrowed her eyes. "Because why?"

"Can't tell you. It's a surprise." Robin grinned.

"Tell me."

"Nope. You'll find out soon enough."

"Tease." Charlotte turned to Ruby. "And you'll keep the pocket so I can put the letter back in it? I want it in the pocket for the wedding."

"Yes, I can do that."

"Well, I think this will be perfect."

"Come, let me get your measurements. I can't wait to get started." Ruby picked up her measuring tape and a pad of paper.

"Mom, you here?" Ben's voice rang through the kitchen.

"Ben, don't come in," Ruby called out. "And make sure to pull that screen door all the way closed."

The dogs, no longer interested in the dress, raced out of the room to greet Ben.

"Why not?" Ben called out.

Robin jumped up. "I've got this. I'll shoo him away. No seeing the bride in her gown before the wedding day. That's bad luck."

"And I don't need any more of that," Charlotte said as she leaned over the table, admiring the rough sketch Ruby had made. She had to admit, she was liking this dress better than her original one.

"Ruby, you sure you'll have the time?"

"I'm certain. And I want to do this for you."

"Thanks, Ruby." She hugged her future mother-in-law. She'd sure won in the mother-in-law department. She felt closer to Ruby now than she ever had with her own mother.

But then family dynamics had always been... complicated with her family.

CHAPTER 4

Charlotte climbed aboard Ben's boat, Lady Belle, later that evening, excited to tell him all the news. All the things that had fallen apart and then just magically fallen into place again. He'd laugh when she told him about making a wish at Lighthouse Point, but she didn't care. *Something* was making things work out now.

"Ben?" She called out as she climbed aboard.

"In here."

She followed his voice and found him in the small galley kitchen. "There you are."

He walked over and gave her a kiss, then wrapped his arms around her. "I missed you."

"You just saw me yesterday."

"I know, it's been forever." His mouth curved in an infectious smile.

She settled into his arms. "So, Christmas music, huh?"

"Just thought I should get in the spirit of things, what with having a holiday wedding and everything."

"Well, I almost had to postpone everything."

Ben pulled back and stared. "What? You don't want to postpone it."

"No, I don't. I didn't. But we lost Charming Inn for a venue and my wedding dress burned up in a fire."

Astonishment covered his features and he sucked in a quick breath. "We're not getting married at the inn?"

"No. I mean yes. I mean… come sit. And hand me that glass of wine I see you poured." They settled onto the settee in the main cabin area.

"Okay, explain."

"So, the inn got double-booked, but then the other person moved their wedding to Magic Cafe… Tally had just had a cancellation for the date."

"That's quite a coincidence."

She laughed. "I thought so."

"And the dress?"

"Your mom is going to make me one. Julie gave me the dress she wore, and your mom is doing her magic. And the dress... it has so much history and this letter in the pocket from this woman, Barbara, who wore it first... I'm just so happy right now." Joy bubbled through her.

"I can tell." He leaned over and kissed her. "So that's what was going on at Mom's when Robin chased me away and said you'd explain."

"Yes, we were working on the design for the dress. And your mom came up with the best design."

"She's talented, isn't she? She really has enjoyed getting back into her dressmaking and designs."

"Now, if we could just find a place to live." She sighed. "I know we haven't found a place yet. I guess we'll just have to shuttle back and forth between my little cottage and Lady Belle until something comes up. But I wish we had a place we could call our own."

"Funny you should say that. Come on, let's take a walk. I have news for you, too. A surprise." Ben's face held a secretive grin.

29

"Where to?"

"Come with me." He stood and held out his hand.

"So, it was very strange." Ben helped her climb off the boat. "Kind of a coincidence, really. But this morning, Len Hoverton came into the marina to ask me to help sell his boat. Said they were moving. You know the Hovertons, right? Well, they have this house on the bay. I've only been in it once, but I remember the light in there is amazing."

They headed down the pier and onto the street. "So I went to go see it today. I think it's perfect for us. The price is right. And Len said his wife was really particular about who moves into it. She loves it so much and wants the new owners to love it as much as she did. They've already moved, he's just back here dealing with getting it freshly painted and to sell his boat. He gave me a key so we could come back this evening and see it."

"Really?" She was almost afraid to get her hopes up.

"You're going to love it." He led the way down a short walk from the marina and stopped in front of a charming yellow two-story house with a large porch out front.

"So far I'm a big fan. It's adorable."

"Just wait until you see inside." He opened the door and led her in.

She stood back and looked around the great room that stretched from the front of the house to the back. The far side of the room was lined with French doors leading outside. They crossed over and Ben opened the door. "Look at that view."

Palm trees framed the view. A sailboat cut across the water. The view really was lovely looking out over the bay.

"And it's close to the marina, which is great for me, and near the point. Just take the beach around the bend and you're at Lighthouse Point."

"Ben, it's gorgeous."

"Come on. You have to see the kitchen, then the bayside room upstairs. It will be perfect for a studio for you. So much natural light."

They explored the kitchen with its soft gray wood cabinets and shiny stainless appliances. It was open and airy, and she loved it.

He led her upstairs to the large room off the landing. She gasped when she saw it. "Oh, Ben. This is perfect."

Windows lined the two exterior walls, one

facing the bay and one the side yard. There would be wonderful light available for her painting.

"You like it, right?" His eyes lit up, hopeful for her approval.

"I love it." She threw herself into his arms. "I never thought we'd find something this wonderful."

"I'm glad you like it because I pretty much told Len we'd take it. I'm going to text him right now."

"You do that while I explore around some more."

There was another guest bedroom upstairs and a hall bath. She headed back downstairs and found the master suite. It was nestled on a corner of the house with a huge bay window with a window seat. The view of the bay beckoned enticingly. She couldn't imagine a more perfect house for them.

Ben clambered down the stairs. "We're all set. We're going to use a real estate attorney to save on fees. Looks like we have ourselves a home."

"We can afford all this?"

"It's right in the price range we discussed."

"I can't believe it." She hugged him again.

They walked out to the expansive deck

overlooking the bay. He threaded his fingers through hers, and they stood there for a few moments in silence.

She turned to him and looked into his eyes. "Hey, Ben. You know what I did yesterday after everything was going wrong for the wedding?"

"What?" He squeezed her hand, his lips tipped in a smile.

"I went to Lighthouse Point and made a wish."

"What did you wish for?" He kissed her lightly on the side of her cheek.

"For everything to be perfect."

He laughed. "Well, so far, so good."

So far, so good indeed.

CHAPTER 5

The next day Lillian looked up from the reception desk at Charming Inn to see Charlotte standing there with a wide grin on her face.

Lillian hurried around the desk to hug her. "So, you heard that the wedding mix-up has been solved."

"Oh, Lil, I'm so happy to be getting married here. You've always made it feel like home to me here at Charming Inn."

"And you and Robin, along with Sara, have always felt like you were my family." She stepped back and released Charlotte but still held her hand. "And Sara told me about your wedding dress problem."

"The one that's no longer a problem?"

"That exact one." Lillian smiled. "I was over having coffee with Ruby this morning and she was already working on your dress. She showed me the sketch and... well, it looks so like you. Simple, flowy, even a bit bohemian." She laughed. "I hope it's okay to call it that."

"Sure, I'm almost a hippie at heart." Charlotte grinned. "I'm actually carrying a wildflower bouquet with different red, white, and a few yellow flowers. We're having simple arrangements of red carnations with baby's breath on the tables at the reception. My mom and sister are going to hate it. They're all about formal rose bouquets."

"But you're not going to worry about their opinions, are you?"

"Nope. I have a new motto these days. Don't listen to the naysayers."

"Great motto to have." Lillian loved that Charlotte was finally standing up to her overbearing mother and sister.

"I came to check on the rooms. You have a suite for my parents and that large corner room for Eva, right?"

"I do."

Charlotte grinned. "I'm sure Eva will have some complaints for you."

"I do like to keep my guests happy, but I might have to just listen to your motto for a bit while they're here." Lillian laughed.

"Good plan. Well, I'm off to go talk to Jay and make sure that everything is set for food for the reception."

"I'm sure it is. You know Jay. Everything will be great."

"I have no doubt."

Charlotte walk away and happiness flowed through Lillian as she went back behind the counter. All *her girls*—as she thought of them —were getting the happiness they deserved. First Sara, then Robin, and now Charlotte. She turned at the sound of someone coming behind the reception desk and smiled when she saw who it was.

"Hello, gorgeous wife." Gary's lips curved with that special smile he had just for her.

"Hello, my handsome husband."

He opened his arms and she walked into his embrace. The embrace that felt like home to her. That made her feel like everything was perfect in her world.

"I love you," he whispered against her ear.

"And I love you. More than I could ever say."

"But I do love hearing you say it."

"I love you." She obliged him by saying it again.

He brushed a lock of her hair away from her face and looked directly into her eyes. "I'll never know why or how I got lucky enough to find you." His eyes sparkled with love.

She settled her face against his chest, listening to his heartbeat, content with her world. Happy for the girls. Happy for herself. Glad she could share Charming Inn with Charlotte for her special day.

CHARLOTTE HURRIED off to the kitchen and found Robin perched on the counter talking with Jay. "Hey, you two."

"Hey, yourself. I was just telling Jay how lucky you've been about your wedding." Robin slid down off the counter and went and grabbed a cup of coffee, pressing it into Charlotte's hands. "Here, you look like you could use this."

"Thank you." She blew on the hot liquid,

anxious to take a sip as soon as it cooled off enough. She leaned against the counter.

"I told him about your wish at Lighthouse Point." Robin's voice held just a tinge of teasing.

"Hey, I believe in wishes at the point." Jay thrust out a spatula for emphasis. "Mine came true." He winked at Robin.

"I'm beginning to believe the legend, too."

"I'm not going to argue with you two. I kind of believe it myself." Robin touched Jay's arm and a special smile crept between them.

Charlotte took a sip of coffee and turned to Jay. "So you have everything ordered and planned for the reception, right? I swear I can't take another mishap."

"I do. Don't worry about a thing. The buffet is going to be just like you wanted. And the champagne for the toasts came in yesterday. We're good, really." Jay worked on cooking a batch of pancakes for Charming Inn's guests as he talked to them.

"Well, that's one thing I won't have to worry about." She took another sip of the coffee. So delicious. Whoever invented coffee was a genius.

"So it looks like everything is a go, right? No more problems?" Robin asked.

"Unless the fact that my sister is coming to town would be considered a problem." She grimaced.

Robin laughed. "Okay, that's a problem, but we'll deal with it. Did you get the final count for the wedding?"

"I did. Left it on your desk in your office. I'm so pleased how it turned out. Just the right size. Friends, family."

"You and Ben have a lot of friends, though." Robin laughed again.

"We do."

"So, you want to go over the decorations one more time? Come to my office with me."

"Sure, I've got time." She turned to Jay. "Thanks again for all your help on food for the wedding."

"Hey, it's my job here at Charming Inn."

"I still appreciate all your help with the choices and the fact that you're a fabulous cook."

Jay grinned. "And I love to hear that. Flattery will get you everywhere." He pointed the spatula toward a plate of cinnamon rolls on the counter. "Take one of those with you to Robin's office."

"If you insist." She grinned and grabbed a roll. "Robin?"

"Nah, I already stole one and finished it." Robin shrugged, a sheepish expression on her face.

They headed to Robin's office and her friend pulled out a file folder. "Okay, we have white Christmas lights that are already strung all along the deck area. We'll have a small Christmas tree decorated in the corner of the deck with lighted boxes under it." Robin nodded. "That was your idea. I know how you love Christmas trees. And we'll have red bows tied along the railing, too."

"It all sounds so magical."

"And if it gets chilly—but it's not supposed to —we'll roll out some patio heaters. Oh, and red bows tied along the aisle chairs for the ceremony out on the beach."

"The florist has a Christmassy floral arrangement for the top of the arbor." Charlotte slowly ticked off things in her mind, hoping she hadn't missed anything.

"And we'll have some solar powered twinkle lights on the arbor, too. Since you're getting married at sunset, I think they'll start to show soon into the ceremony." Robin looked at her list. "I think that's everything?"

"I hope so. I'm ready for this. I can't wait to

be married to Ben." Her pulse quickened at the thought.

"Married life is pretty great." Robin's expression glowed with happiness. "You know, as of the few months I've been an expert at it."

"But you're happy, right?"

"Never been happier."

"I can't believe that when I moved back to Belle Island—and it wasn't long ago—we all were single. Now Sara is married, you're married, and I will be in just a handful of days."

"It does seem a bit strange. Sometimes I feel like we're still those schoolgirls running along the beach, splashing in the waves." Robin closed the file, a pensive look on her face.

"But the island has been good to us, hasn't it?"

"That it has." Robin nodded.

CHAPTER 6

Ben stood in the galley of Lady Belle, cleaning everything, and making sure it was all in tiptop shape. He hoped Charlotte would like her surprise—all of them actually. They planned on taking Lady Belle out for a few days for their honeymoon. But she didn't know he'd arranged for them to anchor off a private island nearby in the gulf. Jay helped him plan for some easy to make but tasty meals for while they were out.

He'd gotten Christmas lights to string on the boat along with a small Christmas tree he was going to put up to surprise her. He hoped he could make their few days of honeymoon special.

They'd considered going away for a week or so, but with it being so close to Christmas and wanting to be home for their first holiday together, they decided a few days out on Lady Belle would be perfect.

Now it looked like they could come home to their new house, too. They'd ordered a bed for their bedroom, and Charlotte had fallen in love with an old, beautiful table for the great room at Bella's vintage shop in town. So, they wouldn't have a lot, but they'd have a place to sleep and sit down to eat. He found some old wooden Adirondack chairs at the marina and painted them a cheerful teal color. He was going to sneak those over to the deck at the new house to surprise Charlotte, too. Luckily Len had let them have access to the house right away by renting it to them until all the paperwork of the sale was finalized.

He'd talked to Sara and Robin and they were helping him with another surprise. It was hard to surprise Charlotte with anything, but he hoped she'd be pleased with all he'd arranged. Truth be told, he was content spending the rest of his life making her happy. Making her happy made *him* happy. He smiled to himself just thinking of the look on her face when she saw everything.

He whistled under his breath as he cleaned

the Lady Belle, making her sparkle for her honeymoon cruise.

A FEW DAYS LATER, Robin met Sara at The Nest, the private area of Charming Inn where Lillian lived. They had plans to make.

"Sara, you here?" Robin called through the screen on the door to the deck.

"In here."

Robin went inside and found Sara in the kitchen.

"I made us some tea." Sara pointed to a pitcher of sweet tea on the counter and two large glasses of ice.

"Perfect." They sat at the kitchen table and Sara pulled out her ever-present notebook.

"Okay, so I found a box of white Christmas lights in Aunt Lillian's storage. Tons of them. We can decorate the deck of Ben and Charlotte's new house with them."

"That's great. She'll need a tree, though. You know how Charlotte loves her Christmas trees."

"I thought we could pick one up at the tree lot as soon as they leave on their honeymoon."

"Sure. Maybe Jay will come along and wrestle it for us. We can use the inn's van to haul it."

"What about decorations for the tree?" Sara tapped her pen.

"That's where I came up with a great idea." Robin set down her glass. "I thought we could ask people at the wedding to write down their wish for Ben and Charlotte. I bought some ornament shaped cutouts. Then we'll hang them on their tree."

"That's a fabulous idea."

"And guess what I found? You know how Charlotte always loved those bubble lights?"

"I remember those."

Robin leaned back with a triumphant smile. "I found some online and ordered them in. I figure a few strands of regular mini-lights, then these."

"Charlotte is going to love this."

"She is. If we can just keep it all a secret from her."

"Keep what a secret from who?" Charlotte entered the kitchen and Sara looked up with a guilty expression.

"Nothing," Robin said quickly.

"Lillian said you two were in here and to just come in. What are you doing?"

"Oh, we were just going over last-minute details for the wedding," Sara said. "Don't worry. We've got it all covered. You have the two best maids of honor in the world."

Robin rushed to cover up what they were actually doing. "Yes, we were working on our best maid—*matron*, I guess—speech. So that needs to be a surprise," she improvised.

"Here, you want some sweet tea?" Sara jumped up, taking her notebook with her.

"Yes, thanks." Charlotte sat down at the table.

"So, did you have another fitting with Ruby?" Robin asked.

"I did and you should see the dress. It's wonderful. Better than anything I'd ever imagined. And it's just so... well, it's so me."

"I'm glad you're happy with it. Kind of a blessing that your other dress was ruined." Sara sat back down.

"Now, if I can just gear up for my family coming here."

"When do they arrive?" Sara asked.

"Tomorrow."

It was hard to miss the look of apprehension on Charlotte's face. "It's going to be fine, Char," Robin assured her.

"Don't let your mother or sister dampen your spirits. It's a wonderful time of your life. You're getting married," Sara added.

"I know. And I'm happy. Really happy. It's just..." Charlotte sighed. "Eva."

"Is she bringing a plus-one?" Robin asked, hoping that if Eva did it might keep her busy with something other than tormenting Charlotte.

"No, not according to her RSVP card."

"You're going to be surrounded by people who love you, so you can just ignore any remarks Eva makes." Sara reached out and touched Charlotte's hand.

"That's easier said than done." Charlotte's eyes clouded with apprehension.

"Eva needs an off switch. She needs to think before she says things." Sara shook her head.

Robin agreed with Sara's take on Eva, but she wanted to sound encouraging. "It's all going to be fine, Char. Just you wait and see."

Robin silently vowed to run as much interference as possible. There was no way Eva was going to spoil Charlotte's big day.

CHAPTER 7

C harlotte walked into Charming Inn the next afternoon, her shoulders set, a smile —if mostly artificial—pasted on her face. Lillian had texted to say her family had arrived. Charlotte had run out of things she just *had* to do before coming to see them. Like clean up her studio and do the dishes and actually fold laundry and put it away. Oh, and she'd washed the kitchen window, too. Had to be done. She'd swear it.

She rolled her eyes at herself. It was ridiculous to let her sister and her mother affect her like this. She'd planned the perfect wedding to marry a man she loved with her whole heart. Nothing should spoil that. Nothing.

"There you are, Charlotte." Eva's voice rang out across the lobby of Charming Inn.

"Hi, Eva. Mom. Dad." She gave her father a hug.

"Good to see you." Her father held her for a moment before releasing her. "So, how's the bride-to-be?"

"I'm doing great, Dad." At least she had one supporter in the family.

She turned to her mother. "How are you doing, Mother? Have a nice trip in?"

"I do hate that we can't get a direct flight here. It's ridiculous the tortuous route we have to take. It's like you're in the middle of nowhere. I'm sure your wedding guests won't like how difficult it is to get here either." Her mother's brow creased with a disapproving frown.

Probably not the last of those frowns she'd be seeing this weekend. So it began.

"Most of the guests will be from in town."

"Right, because you refused to let us invite Father's business associates like would have been appropriate." Eva rolled her eyes.

"Ben and I wanted a smaller wedding. Just family and close friends." But her sister knew that.

"I'm sure it will be perfect." Her father nodded encouragingly. "So where is the groom?"

"He got tied up at the marina, but he'll join us at Magic Cafe for dinner."

"You did ask for inside seating this time, didn't you?" Eva let out a long, put-upon sigh.

"Ah... no. I asked for a large table right by the beach. The sunset promises to be gorgeous tonight and I thought we could enjoy it out on the deck."

"The wind from the beach will make your hair go all wild." Eva shook her head. "I don't understand your fascination with eating outside."

"Eva, we had a conversation about... you know." Her father broke in on Eva's stream of criticism. "Let's all be supportive, shall we?"

She stared at her father for a moment for his welcome but unexpected intervention and sent him a grateful look.

"Are you all ready to go? We could walk," she suggested.

"Oh, no. We'll take the car we rented. It's way too far to walk." Her mother countered her suggestion with a frown. Again.

Should she count the frowns tonight?

Okay, a ride it was. They headed to Magic

Cafe and pulled into the crushed shell parking lot. Eva looked at the lot in disdain but thankfully didn't say anything as she gingerly walked across the surface.

"So glad to have you back again. Glen, Isadora, welcome. And Eva, good to see you." Tally's cheerful voice welcomed them. "And Charlotte, our bride-to-be." Tally hugged her.

"Tally, glad to be back here at your lovely restaurant. I hear we have a table out by the beach." Her father's tone held a bit of a warning note for Eva as he glanced over at her.

They followed Tally to their beachside table where Ben was waiting for them. He jumped up when he saw them and stretched out a hand to her father.

"Glen, glad you got here."

"Ben, my boy. Great to see you." He pumped Ben's hand.

"Isadora, Eva, hi." He turned to the women.

"Benjamin." Her mother slipped into the chair her father held out for her and Eva sat down beside her.

She sat beside Ben, and he squeezed her leg beneath the table. It was going to be fine.

Everything was. Because Ben was here by her side, right?

BEN CAREFULLY KEPT a pleasant expression on his face, steeling himself for the first criticism he was sure to get from Eva or Isadora. At least Charlotte's father seemed to like him.

But they were all Charlotte's family and he vowed that he'd win them over.

Or die trying.

Which might actually be what happened.

They ordered drinks—he ordered a cold beer for fortitude—and the conversation turned to the wedding. Charlotte sat unusually quiet by his side. He reached over and held her hand, squeezing it in support. She turned and sent him a grateful smile.

"So, Mother and I did like that gown you chose. The one you sent pictures of. Not quite as classic as we hoped, but at least it had a nice cut to it." Eva sipped her chardonnay.

"About that. That dress got ruined."

"Oh, no. I hope you didn't have to just get

one off the rack. That just wouldn't do." Isadora frowned.

"No, Ruby is making a dress for me. A friend, Julie, gave me the dress she wore. It has all this history and Ruby is redesigning it bit."

"A homemade dress?" Eva frowned in a twin frown to their mother's.

"A custom dress. Designed just for me. And it's... well, it's perfect."

"My mom's a very talented seamstress. She's made quite a few wedding dresses in the last few months. Seems like everyone is getting married on Belle Island these days."

Eva gave him a doubtful look.

"I'm sure you'll look beautiful," her father said.

At least Glen was being supportive. That was good.

"And you have everything else planned, right? You didn't miss any of the details?" her mother questioned.

"No, I didn't miss anything. Flowers, food for the reception, and decorations."

"I hope you didn't go overboard with the whole Christmas theme. That's just so... overdone." Eva shook her head.

Ben glanced at Charlotte, wondering if she was going to explain their Christmas lights and red bow theme or just let Eva figure it out when she saw it.

"Yes, it's Christmassy. I love Christmas. We'll have white Christmas lights and red bows and lots of greenery. I think it's going to look like a Christmas wonderland. Robin and Sara are helping me with it."

"You didn't get a wedding planner?" Isadora frowned again.

He briefly wondered if the woman would get permanent frown lines from all her disapproval this weekend.

"No, just Robin and Sara. We did it all."

"Well... I certainly hope it turns out okay. I hope it's not an embarrassment." Eva shook her head.

Ben squeezed Charlotte's hand. Hard. "I think it's going to be wonderful. Exactly what Charlotte has dreamed about."

"If you say so." Eva turned and started to peruse the menu.

Charlotte sent him another grateful look. He leaned close and whispered, "It will be wonderful."

Isadora's phone went off and she looked at it. "Oh, I must take this. It's the woman I left in charge of the Snow Gala. You know it's next weekend, right? I really shouldn't be out of town right now so close to the gala. It's a lot of work to coordinate it."

"I know, Mother. This wedding really is at the most inconvenient time." Eva looked up from the menu.

Isadora chatted away with the lady while they all looked at the menu. Not that he needed a menu at Magic Cafe. He had it memorized from the millions of times he'd been here. But looking at it gave him something to do while Isadora chattered on, oblivious to the glares of other diners as her loud voice circled around the tables near them.

Isadora finally ended her call. "So many problems. I really should be there."

"I'm sure it will all be fine. You can sort it out next week when we get home," Glen said. "Now, let's order. Love the food here. Been waiting for Tally's blackened fish since the last time we were here."

Somehow they got through the meal without Charlotte reaching over and strangling her sister.

Charlotte's family headed out in their car and he offered to walk Charlotte home.

They stood by the entranceway to Magic Cafe and waved to her family. As soon as they were gone, he tugged Charlotte into his arms and kissed her.

She kissed him back, sighed, then pulled back. "What was that for?"

"Because you're an amazing woman. And I love you."

"I'm amazing because I didn't pour my drink on my sister's head?"

He laughed. "Don't pay any attention to her. We're going to have a fabulous wedding."

"On the bright side, there's only the rehearsal tomorrow, then the wedding, then they'll go back to Austin." She kissed him quickly on the cheek. "And you're a saint to listen to all of that."

Ben had to admit he was grateful for his own family. So supportive. He adored his mother. And his mother adored Charlotte. At least they had that.

"How about we go to Lady Belle and have a drink?" Charlotte suggested.

"I... uh... she's a mess. I have everything thrown around getting ready for the wedding."

He didn't want her to see all the decorating he'd started doing on the boat. "How about we go to your cottage?"

"Sure, that's fine." She slid her hand in his, and they headed down the sidewalk to her cottage. She was thankfully oblivious to his little white lie. And it was a bit messy on Lady Belle right now, so it wasn't *really* an untruth.

CHARLOTTE SANK onto the loveseat next to Ben and handed him a glass of wine. He held up his glass. "To only two nights before you're my wife."

They clinked glasses and she leaned back against him, letting the stress of the evening slowly slip away.

"You did a good job handling your sister and your mother's remarks." Ben shifted slightly and slid an arm around her.

"Did you see how many times Mother frowned? I was counting them, but finally decided it was too many to count."

Ben grinned.

"Anyway, they are who they are. And I just

have this feeling that no matter what happens, the wedding is going to be perfect," Charlotte said. Ever since she'd made that wish on Lighthouse Point things had started falling together. The wedding was back at Charming Inn. She had the most beautiful wedding dress ever. They'd found a house to live in. What could possibly go wrong now? She had faith in her small little shell. So far it had been working its magic.

"You know, Char, you've been the best thing that's ever happened to me. You're my best friend and I swear you know me better than anyone else. I can't imagine my life without you in it." Ben pulled her closer.

"Oh, Ben, I feel the same way. So lucky to have found you. I can't wait to become your wife." Even her mother and sister couldn't put a shadow on her mood tonight. Her heart sang with happiness.

"We've got this. You and me together. Just two more days." He kissed her cheek and she settled against him, secure in his love.

CHAPTER 8

The next morning Robin stood in the kitchen and flinched as Jay slammed down the phone in the kitchen at the inn.

"What's wrong?"

"That was the new supplier I've been using. They messed up the order. I don't have enough of the chicken for the chicken parmesan for Charlotte's wedding. This is the second and last time they get to screw up my order. I'm looking for a new supplier." Jay raked his hand through his hair. "I'm going to have to go to the mainland and source some more.

"I'd ride along, but I have so much to still do to get ready for the wedding. Plus we have the rehearsal, too."

"Right, I still need to deal with the rehearsal dinner, too." Jay sighed.

"Let me help." Dana, Jay's assistant, walked up to them. "I can go to the mainland or work on the rehearsal food."

Robin looked at Jay, wondering if he'd actually allow Dana to take on something like this. She'd been working out really well. If only Jay could turn over a few of his responsibilities.

Jay looked at Dana and nodded slowly. "I have the plans for the rehearsal pinned up over there." He pointed to the bulletin board. "The bottom shelf in the fridge has what I've already started. And we're having an ice cream sundae buffet for dessert. Ben wanted that." Jay shrugged. "And he got his way."

Robin laughed. "Charlotte was willing to go with about anything Ben wanted on the rehearsal dinner if he let her have her say on the actual wedding food."

Dana stepped over to the bulletin board. "I'll keep going on the rehearsal food. I already have lunch under control. I'll call in an extra kitchen hand or two."

"Thanks, Dana." Robin nodded encouragingly to the girl.

"Okay, I'm going to grab the van keys and I'm out of here. Call if you have any questions at all, Dana."

"I will."

Jay left and Robin turned to Dana. "Well, that was surprising."

"I know. He's giving me more and more responsibility all the time. Maybe he'll even take a day off someday." Dana grinned.

"Wouldn't that be nice?" Robin smiled, doubting it would happen. Her husband worked long, hard hours. But then so did she. But she got to go home to him every night and they were blissfully happy. What more could a couple want? A bottomless sense of peace and satisfaction surged through her as she went off to work on decorations for tonight's rehearsal dinner.

ROBIN AND LILLIAN stood in the lobby going over the checklist for the rehearsal this evening. Robin looked up to see Delbert Hamilton and Camille Montgomery headed toward them. Great, just what they needed. But she pasted a welcoming —hopefully convincing—smile on her face.

"Delbert, Camille. How nice to see you." Robin hoped her tone was welcoming enough.

"We have reservations here for the weekend." Camille let out a long sigh. "Mama has rented out our home here for the weekend. I keep telling her that she should stop renting it out. I mean, what if we need it for some reason and it's not available? Just like this weekend. It's just so... *inconvenient.*"

Delbert smiled, seemingly ignoring Camille's complaints. "We have reservations here for the weekend. Two suites."

"Yes, I saw you on the reservation list." Lillian shook Del's outreached hand. "We're so glad to have you staying with us."

"We're here for Ben's wedding and I do need to pop over to Moonbeam Bay and check on how the renovations are going on The Cabot Hotel there. Staying here just makes all that easier." He winked. "Plus, you know I adore your lovely inn."

Lillian smiled. "Thank you. Why don't you come this way and I'll get you checked in?"

Delbert left with Lillian, and Camille turned to Robin. "So... another wedding here. I just do not get the... allure. It's so... rustic."

"I'd hardly call the inn rustic. It's... lovely.

And charming. And—" She stopped. There was no convincing Camille, so why bother?

"And why people insist on outside weddings. It's so humid and just... well, there are bugs, too." Camille shook her head, her perfectly curled hair bouncing about her shoulders.

"Charlotte's wedding is going to be incredible. Wonderful. Enchanting." She wondered if her smile was beginning to fade.

"Delbert insisted on coming because he and Ben have become friends. Why, I'll never fathom. They are so... different." Camille frowned.

She looked honestly perplexed on how a man who ran a chain of luxury hotels and a man who ran a marina could become friends.

"Camille—you—"

Delbert came back just in time to keep Robin from saying something she shouldn't.

"Camille, darlin', let's go on up to our rooms. We'll get all unpacked. Then we'll head on over to Moonbeam Bay."

"Delbert, I think I'll just stay here. I don't really feel like the drive. Though I don't know what I'll do to keep occupied here at the inn."

A beach walk? A light lunch? A drink at the

outside bar? Read? But Robin just kept her ever-fading smile and said nothing.

Delbert and Camille left to go up to their rooms and Robin let her face relax. She looked down at where she was clutching the to-do list. It was now a wrinkled wad of paper from her grip.

Ah, well.

She'd just do her best to avoid Camille while she was here. Steering clear of Camille was always the best plan.

CHAPTER 9

Charlotte had managed to avoid her family all day by coming up with an amazingly long list of things she needed to do. At first, she'd been worried that her mother or Eva would offer to help... but that didn't happen. They were headed off for a shopping day in Sarasota.

She spent the day just pampering herself with a new manicure and a luxurious soak in the tub. She'd put those things on a list, though, so they should both count toward her amazingly long list of to-dos, right?

She put on the new dress she'd bought for the rehearsal tonight. A simple, flowing dress that hit a bit below her knees. She twirled around once, like a little girl, smiling at the skirt billowing around her. The dress was a rich blue color with tiny flecks of white in it, and she loved it. She was pretty sure her mother wouldn't approve, though. Her mother would come in some extravagant fitted dress with a matching jacket if she had to guess.

She'd twisted her hair back in a loose braid with just a smattering of locks framing her face. A touch of makeup, a bit of almost nude lipstick, and she called it good.

She grabbed a white sweater with dainty pearl buttons from a hanger in the closet in case it got chilly. With one more spin in front of the mirror and a silly, self-satisfied smile, she headed for the kitchen. She stared at the car keys on the counter and debated driving. She bit her lip. Should she drive? Did she have enough time to walk there? Yes. She decided to walk. She wanted to linger and enjoy every single minute of tonight and tomorrow.

She locked the door, stepped outside, and laughed. "Well, hi there."

Ben came up the walkway and gave her a kiss. "Figured you'd be walking over."

She slid her hand in his, feeling the warmth of his grip. Yes, she was going to enjoy every single moment of the next few days with this man she adored. "You know me so well."

"I do." He kissed her again, then they headed off for Charming Inn at a leisurely pace.

LILLIAN WALKED into the kitchen at Charming Inn just to check and make sure everything was going as planned for Charlotte's rehearsal dinner. Dana was rushing around, trying to manage everything, and there was no sign of Jay.

Robin came walking out of the storeroom, an apron tied around her nice outfit, obviously already dressed for the rehearsal. She carried a tray of food and set it on the counter.

"Where's Jay?" Lillian asked.

"He went to the mainland to get things he needs for the wedding tomorrow. His supplier shorted him."

"Then, hand me an apron."

Robin reached over to a hook and handed one to her. She tied it over her nice dress and was glad she'd decided on flats for the rehearsal tonight. "Dana, put me to work."

Dana gave her a few jobs to do while Robin chipped in where she could.

She looked up later when Jay slammed through the kitchen door, an exasperated look plastered on his face.

"Got the supplies." He swung a large cooler into the kitchen. "Another cooler in the van. Be right back."

He returned with another huge rolling cooler, then glanced at the clock on the wall. "I don't have much time."

Dana hurried over. "I'll put this in the fridge. You go change. Can't have the best man being late for the rehearsal."

"I can't leave you with all this."

"Of course you can. You go be best man. I've got all this. We're almost ready with the food for the dinner tonight. After that is served, I'm going to do more for the wedding prep. It's all fine."

Robin nodded at Jay, pushing him gently toward the door. "Do as she says. Go grab a quick shower. You only have about thirty minutes."

Jay didn't look convinced, but he hurried out of the kitchen. Gary peeked his head in. "Everything okay in here?"

"If by okay, you mean... not really?" Robin pushed back a damp lock of hair.

Gary entered the kitchen, grabbed an apron, and turned to Lillian and Dana. "Put me to work."

"You sure?" Lillian looked gratefully at her husband.

"I'm sure. Not much of a cook, but I can follow directions."

"Perfect. Dana's good with directions." Lillian turned to Robin. "You should go see if Charlotte is here yet. If nothing else, you can run interference between her and her sister."

"You sure you've got this?"

"We do. Go be the matron of honor."

"Or half-matron." Robin smiled as she took off her apron and straighten her dress. "But I will go find Char." She hurried out of the kitchen.

Gary leaned over and kissed her. "Put me to work."

And with that, Dana started dividing tasks and they all went to work making sure everything was perfect for Charlotte's rehearsal dinner.

CHAPTER 10

R obin thought Jay looked particularly handsome standing up by Ben as the best man. Jay had on a white, button-down shirt and black slacks. Very different than his usual t-shirt and jeans attire. Yes, he did look handsome. Very.

He looked over and saw her staring and winked, an impish grin on his face. She grinned back at him, then turned to concentrate on the rehearsal. That's why they were here. Not to just stand and gawk at her handsome husband.

Ruby's husband, David, was also a groomsman. She was glad to see that David and Ben had worked out their differences and were best of friends now.

Charlotte, her cheeks flushed and her eyes

glowing, followed the directions that the minister gave. Her friend was having a simple ceremony and it suited the happy couple perfectly.

"I can't believe there's no wedding coordinator." Eva's voice crossed the distance to where Robin was standing up by Charlotte.

Charlotte glanced her sister's direction, but then turned back and smiled at Ben.

Perfect. Charlotte wasn't going to let Eva get to her. They ran through the basics of the ceremony. Ben made a big show of kissing the bride-to-be. They all laughed and headed up to the large deck for the dinner.

Ben had an arm protectively around Charlotte. He was probably trying to run interference just like she was.

Jay appeared at her side and kissed her cheek. "So, by tomorrow, all three of you will be married women."

"We will." She glanced over to where Sara stood talking to Zoe, Noah's niece, and Mason, Gary's son. Everybody was like one big family here on the island. And she loved that. Loved it a lot.

She took Jay's hand. "Come on. Let's see if we can keep Eva busy and away from Char."

LILLIAN CAME WALKING up to Charlotte, Robin, and Sara after most of the guests had left that evening. She carried a package wrapped in white tissue paper with a red bow on it.

"Charlotte, this is for you."

Charlotte reached for the package and slowly unwrapped it. "Oh, Lillian. It's lovely." She held up a delicate lace knit wrap.

"Just in case it gets chilly tomorrow evening after the wedding."

"See, I told you that the strapless gown would work perfectly." Robin grinned.

"You knew about this?"

"Of course. Lillian has been knitting on it every chance she gets. You know how those Yarnies get."

"The Yarnies even met an extra time last week at the community center while I finished up the wrap," Lillian nodded.

"Well, I love it." Charlotte draped it around her shoulders. "It's just beautiful and will look wonderful with my dress."

"I'm glad you like it."

Ben joined them. "That's pretty."

"Lillian made it." She spun around, showing off the wrap. Okay, and she just liked to spin in the dress and see it swirl around her.

"You about ready to go? Looks like everyone else is gone." Ben grinned at her spinning antics.

"Yes, I'm ready. I guess I should try and get some sleep tonight." She turned and hugged Lillian. "Thank you so much."

"You're welcome."

"And I'll see you two tomorrow." She hugged her friends, then turned to take Ben's hand.

She and Ben slowly walked back to her cottage. The stars twinkled above, and the almost-full moon shone down, spreading silvery light around them. Yes, she was enjoying every moment of this evening.

Ben held her hand in his, squeezing it occasionally. She leaned against him and wrapped her arm around his as they walked.

"It was a wonderful evening, wasn't it?" She glanced up.

"It was."

"I know you and Robin were running interference between Eva and me all night."

"Might have been." He chuckled softly.

"I just ignored almost everything she said."

"She wasn't impressed by the ice cream sundae bar, was she?"

"No, she thought we should have had some kind of fancy petit fours or something. And announced it loudly to anyone who would listen. But did you see how everyone enjoyed the ice cream?"

"I did. Good choice to have Jay get the ice cream from Parker's over in Moonbeam Bay. They have the best ice cream. It was delicious."

"And Jay had so many toppings. It was hard to choose." She laughed.

"It was. So I made two sundaes." Ben grinned as they climbed the stairs to her cottage.

She stood on the top step while he stood one below her so they were face-to-face. He reached out and ran a finger along her jaw and she pressed his hand against her cheek. "I can't wait to be your wife."

"I can't wait to be your husband. We're going to have the best life together."

"We are."

He leaned in and kissed her gently and she wound her arms around his neck, pulling him close. She could stay like this forever.

He finally pulled away. "I should head back to Lady Belle."

"And I should go in." But she didn't really want him to leave.

He kissed her once more, then turned and disappeared down the sidewalk. She stepped inside and walked through the darkened house to her bedroom. She sank onto the bed and kicked off her shoes.

One more night of being single. She didn't know how she'd gotten to this point. It seemed like just the other day she was a young girl racing on the beach with Sara and Robin.

But tomorrow... tomorrow was her wedding day. She glanced at the clock beside her bed. No, *today* was her wedding day. She better get to bed and get some sleep. She smiled as she got up, gave one last spin in her dress, then got ready for bed.

CHAPTER 11

C harlotte headed over to Charming Inn late the next morning. She had nervous energy to burn. It seemed like the minutes were crawling by and it was an eternity until sunset and her wedding. She might as well walk a bit, and then she could check on things at the inn. Though she was sure Robin and Lillian had everything under control.

Then, late this afternoon she was meeting Robin and Sara at The Nest to get ready, but for now... walking seemed like a good choice.

She strolled along the streets in no hurry, and many of the townspeople wished her well on her wedding day. Small towns. Gotta love them.

Everyone knew everything that was going on, and her wedding was no exception. She basked in the well wishes as she walked and tilted her face to the warm sunshine under beautiful blue skies. *Perfect* weather. She laughed. By now she couldn't imagine anything *not* being perfect on this day.

She walked into Charming Inn and headed to the kitchen. Jay was busy with wedding preparations and Robin sipped coffee while he worked.

"Char, what are you doing here?" Robin came over and hugged her.

"I was... I don't know. I just needed to get out and walk."

"Here, have some coffee." Robin handed her a cup. "Do you want something to eat?"

"Nah, I grabbed a piece of toast at home. I'm a bit too nervous to eat much."

"Worried nervous?"

"Just... nervous energy excitement nervous."

The outside door to the kitchen swung open and Julie from The Sweet Shoppe popped her head in. "Anyone here want a wedding cake?"

"I cleared off an area over there." Jay pointed with a long-handled spoon.

"Okay, be right in with it." Julie disappeared out the door.

"I can't wait to see it." Charlotte set down her cup and walked over to the doorway.

Julie and her helper came slowly walking up to the doorway, carefully balancing the cake on a platform between them. Just as they got to the doorway, Julie stumbled, tripping on the step.

In slow-motion horror, the cake started slipping off the platform.

"No!" Julie yelled.

"Watch out." Robin rushed forward, her arms extended.

But the cake didn't listen.

It slowly tumbled to the ground in a mound of icing and crumbles of cake.

Julie bounded up from the ground where she'd fallen. "No." She stood like a statute, mortified. "This has never happened before."

Charlotte looked at her gorgeous cake smashed on the ground. Her heart tightened as she looked at the mess. So much for her perfect day. Disappointment surged through her. She took a breath and slowly swiveled to look at Julie. "Well... okay, then. What's our next option?"

"I am so, so sorry."

"Accidents happen." She tried to sound upbeat—not that she was feeling that way—as she stared at the ruined cake.

"But your cake." Julie dropped to the ground beside the mounds of broken cake and tiny smashed poinsettias made out of icing.

Well, bad things came in threes, right? The venue, the dress, and now the cake. So... she should be good to go from now on out. Except... no cake.

They all stood and looked down at the smashed cake.

"This has *never* happened before," Julie repeated with a look of disbelief in her eyes.

"You okay? You fell pretty hard," Robin asked.

"I'm fine." Julie brushed some icing off her pants and looked at her watch. "I just don't think there's time to replicate this." She turned to Charlotte. "I don't know what to say. I'm so, so sorry."

Charlotte looked down at the ruined cake. "Well... I'm sure it was beautiful?"

"It was." Julie nodded, her eyes sad.

Ruby came walking into the kitchen. "Oh, no. What happened?"

"I tripped," Julie stared down at the mess.

"I'll get this cleaned up. But we need to figure out dessert for the wedding." Jay walked over with a trash bag.

"I have dozens and dozens of fancy Christmas cookies made for an event on Monday. Some still need to be decorated, but I'd have time to do that. You could have them and I'll make more for Monday's event." Julie frowned. "But that won't give you a cake to cut."

Ruby took Charlotte's hand. "Yes, you need a wedding cake to cut. Even a simple one. How about you leave that up to The Yarnies? We'll come up with one. It won't be as big and fancy as Julie's, but you'll have a cake to cut."

"That would be perfect." Charlotte nodded. "And Julie, I'm sure the Christmas cookies will be wonderful. I've seen some of them at The Sweet Shoppe this season. They are works of art. I'm good with that."

"Are you sure? I'm so sorry," Julie apologized yet again.

"I'm sure. It will be fine. The actual wedding is the important part."

Ruby squeezed her hand. "You're a smart woman, Charlotte. That is what's important." Ruby took out her phone. "I'm going to call Dorothy."

"Jay, let me at least help you clean up this mess." Julie looked down at the smashed cake with disbelief still hovering in her eyes.

"No, Dana and I will get this. Sounds like you have a lot of cookie decorating to do."

Ruby walked back over and gave the thumbs up. "Dorothy is already getting things out as we speak. She's a whiz at baking. We'll come up with something for them to have to cut. You get the rest of the cookies ready."

Julie and her helper hurried away.

Robin came up and hugged Charlotte. "You sure you're okay with this?"

"I actually am. I guess I should be upset... but... well, that's the way the cake crumbles." She grinned.

Ruby laughed. "I guess I'm off to make a cake."

"I really appreciate that, Ruby. You sure you have time?"

"I do. And if I start running late, Dorothy said she'd finish it and bring it over."

"Hopefully she won't drop it." Robin grinned. "Oh, too soon?"

"A bit." Charlotte laughed.

"Oh, I was going to bring your dress over here to The Nest for you to get ready. I got it all pressed this morning."

"I'll go pick it up. I have time," Charlotte insisted. Besides, it would keep her busy until it was time to get ready.

"Okay, you know where the key is."

Probably half the island knew that Ruby kept a key under the flowerpot by her door.

Ruby left and Charlotte turned to Robin. "I guess I'll head over to Ruby's and get the dress. I'll go to the cottage first and grab my car, then head over. I'll meet you back here about three?"

"Sounds good. Three it is."

Charlotte hurried out of the inn and back into the bright sunshine. She felt like she *should* feel bad about the cake. And she did… kind of. Julie had obviously spent a long time making it perfect. But she just wasn't that upset, and she thought the Christmas cookies would go along nicely with their whole Christmas theme. Though, she was sure to hear about it from Eva.

But she actually didn't care what Eva thought.

And she smiled at that decision as she headed down the sidewalk, still certain that everything was going to be perfect.

CHAPTER 12

Charlotte grabbed a shower, then put together a bag with things she would need to get ready for the wedding. Robin was going to do her hair up for her in a fancy bun. Robin was good at that.

She had her shoes. Red ones. It just seemed fitting. She got her makeup and the earrings she wanted to wear. After grabbing a few more things, she put the bag in her car. She'd go get the dress and meet her friends at The Nest.

Because she was getting married. *Today.* She skipped out to the car like a young schoolgirl as happiness thrummed through her.

She headed over and pulled into the driveway of Ruby's house. She bounded up the stairs and got the key from under the planter, opened the door, and headed inside.

She was greeted by Mischief and May. The dogs were excited to see her. She put her phone down on the table and leaned down to pet them. After numerous puppy kisses, she stood back up.

"So, it looks like you two are excited about today, too." They wagged their tails in agreement.

She headed to the dining room where Ruby said she'd left the dress. It was hanging in a clear plastic garment bag, and she paused to admire it again. It had turned out so lovely. She grabbed the bag and headed back to the kitchen.

"See you later, pups." She looked around for the dogs. "Pups?"

She carefully placed the dress on the table, making sure not to wrinkle it, and turned around. "Mischief? May? Where are you?"

She had a horrible thought and went over to where she'd left only the screen door closed, not the exterior door.

And the screen door wasn't closed all the way. She glanced outside and there, way down the beach, she saw the puppies racing down the shore.

The memory of Robin chasing after Barney flashed through her mind. What is it with dogs and running off here on Belle Island? Always running away at the worst possible moment.

She spied their leashes hanging by the back door and grabbed them, pushing the screen door and letting it slam behind her. She had to get those pups.

Her heart pounding, she raced down the beach in the direction she'd last seen them.

"I WONDER WHAT'S KEEPING CHARLOTTE?" Robin glanced at the clock on the wall.

"She's probably just taking longer to get her things together. I'm sure she'll be here soon. She's only ten minutes late." Sara stood with her in the extra bedroom at The Nest.

Lillian poked her head in the door. "Gary got ready early and I sent him off so you girls could have The Nest to yourselves. I'm going to check on a few things at the inn, then I'll come back and slip on my dress."

"Okay, let me know if you need help with anything," Robin offered.

"I'm sure you'll have your hands full with getting Charlotte ready. Where is she?"

"Running late. I think I'll text her." Robin grabbed her phone and sent a text.

"Okay, well, I'll be back in a while. Just want to make sure everything is ready for the wedding." Lillian left.

Robin stared at her phone, waiting for Charlotte to return her text. When Charlotte hadn't answered in five minutes, she picked up the phone and called her. Charlotte didn't pick up.

Robin frowned. "Okay, now I'm getting worried. She's not answering her phone."

"Think we have a runaway bride?" Sara laughed.

"No way. She can't wait to marry Ben."

"I'm sure she'll be here soon," Sara said, her voice confident.

"Yes, right. I'm sure you're right." *Maybe.*

By three forty-five Robin was worried. "Maybe Char went to see Ben?"

"Possibly. Why don't you text him?"

"I don't want to worry him."

Sara walked over to her. "I'm starting to get worried no matter how upbeat I've been trying to sound for you. I can't imagine what's keeping her."

"Okay, I'm texting Ben." She tapped a text to him and sank onto the bed, waiting for him to reply. Her phone rang.

"No, Charlotte's not with me. She's supposed to be with you." He sounded worried.

"Yes... well... she's supposed to be here. But she's not."

"How late is she?"

Robin glanced at her watch. "Almost an hour. And she's not answering her phone or texts."

"I'll call you back."

Robin jumped off the bed and paced back and forth, walking to the window and looking outside. Sara came to stand beside her and put an arm around her waist. "I'm sure everything is fine."

"I just can't imagine what is keeping Charlotte from coming to get ready for her wedding."

Her phone rang and she answered it. "Ben?"

"She's not answering me either. And Mom hasn't heard from her but is headed back to the house to get ready. Charlotte was supposed to pick up her dress before meeting you two. I'm going to head there now."

"Okay, call me if you find out anything." She

turned to Sara. "No one's seen her... so don't tell me everything is fine." She glared at Sara even though she knew it wasn't her fault.

"No, I don't think everything is fine anymore. This is not like Charlotte at all." Sara's face looked just as worried as she was now.

CHAPTER 13

Charlotte raced after the dogs, the leashes clutched in her hand. Silly dogs. Why now? And why hadn't she thought to make sure the screen door was closed all the way? It was her fault they got out. She had to find them.

She slowed when she saw a couple walking toward her. "Have you seen two dogs?"

The lady pointed down the beach. "Sure did. They were headed that way."

"Okay, thanks." She sprinted down the beach until she got so winded that she had to stop for a moment. She bent, gulping in large breaths. When she finally could breathe, she stood and put a hand up to shield her eyes from the sun. She looked way down the beach and saw not one sign of the pups.

This was not how she had planned to spend her wedding afternoon. She better call in help or she'd never get to her wedding on time. She reached into her pocket for her phone.

But it wasn't there.

She thought back and sighed when she remembered she'd set it on the counter at Ruby's. Should she go back to Ruby's and call for help? Or keep chasing after the dogs? Just then a bark drifted over from near the tree line a little ways down the beach. She sprinted toward it, hoping it was the missing pups.

How long had she been out here searching? She was never going to have enough time to get ready. But she had to find the pups. Had to.

BEN HURRIED into his mother's house, concern flooding through him. "Mom, you here?"

"I'm here." She hurried into the kitchen.

"Any sign of Charlotte?"

"No, and the dress is still here. See? I don't know what happened. But she was here because the dress was in the dining room where I was working on it, and now it's on the kitchen table."

"I'm going to call her again." Ben tried unsuccessfully to tamp down his worry. There had to be a simple explanation, right? She wouldn't just leave. He chased away all thoughts of any movie he'd seen and story he'd heard of runaway brides.

He dug out his phone and called Charlotte. He whirled around at the sound of a phone ringing. He knew that ring tone. It was a popular sailor tune that Charlotte used for his ringtone as an ode to his love of all things boaty.

His mother frowned and picked up the wedding dress from the table. He snatched up the ringing phone.

"She doesn't go anywhere without her phone." He frowned. "You sure she's not here?"

"I looked everywhere. Each room."

Ruby frowned. "I was so worried about Charlotte... but where are Mischief and May? Mischief? May?" she called out. "Ben, go up and check my closet. They've accidentally gotten shut in there before."

He bounded up the stairs. No dogs. No Charlotte. He checked each closet for good measure and looked under the beds. He clambered back downstairs.

"So unless she's a runaway bride who also stole your dogs... you think the dogs got out and she went after them?"

"That has to be it." His mother nodded. "We need to go find them."

"Okay, I'm going to call Robin and let her know. Then let's get some help and find them."

He called Robin who said she was going to look around the beach at Charming Inn.

"I'll head toward Lighthouse Point. You head the other way. Call if you find her."

His mother headed one direction as he loped down the beach toward Lighthouse Point. He wouldn't feel right until he set his eyes on Charlotte.

CHAPTER 14

C harlotte spied the dogs by the walkway to the lighthouse. Relief washed through her until she realized she had to actually *catch* them before she could be relieved.

She called their names, glad to see they'd at least slowed down on their mad dash to wherever they thought they were going. She got to the walkway, hardly noticing it was decorated for Christmas with bows and lights. She walked slowly so they wouldn't think she was chasing them—though, of course, she was. All she could think of was reaching the pups.

And there, in the middle of the walkway, sat Mischief and May with innocent expressions on their faces, their tails wagging. She slowly approached them until she got close enough to snag their collars. She quickly snapped on their leashes and sank down on the walkway beside them, grateful she'd found them and they hadn't gotten hurt.

She took in big gulps of air, trying to catch her breath and settle her pounding heart.

"Bad dogs, bad dogs." She said in a gentle voice as she hugged them. "So bad." She petted them and cuddled them and waited to finish catching her breath.

She finally stood and led the pups out to the beach to head back to Ruby's. She was never going to get ready on time. Never. Not that she had a clue what time it was because no phone and she hadn't put a watch on today.

She got to the water's edge. Mischief was slowing down. "You need me to carry you, pup? I bet you're tired." She leaned down and petted the dog.

At the sound of her name, she whirled around. Ben raced up to her and gathered her into his arms. "There you are." He held her tight.

She sank into his embrace. "Am I glad to see you."

He stepped back and looked her over carefully. "You okay?"

"I'm fine." She glanced at the dogs. "These two? They aren't on the top of my list right now."

"They got out?"

"I must not have closed the screen door all the way when I went in. So it's my fault. But wow, can these dogs run."

"That Mischief is a little escape artist and May tries to keep up with him."

She looked down at them and shoved her hair out of her face. "Well, now I'm a mess. We're way down here by the lighthouse and I'm not going to have enough time to get ready. I stood right here and I wished for everything to be perfect... and now look at this." She sighed. "I don't think *anyone* could call this perfect."

Ben whipped out his phone. "I've got this. It's still going to be perfect. Sit down for a minute and rest." He grinned. "And don't let go of those leashes."

He stepped away and she saw him talking on his phone. She sat and absentmindedly stroked Mischief's head. The dog leaned against her, oblivious to the commotion he'd caused. May lay down beside her and put her head in her lap. She should really be jumping up and hurrying off. But it was kind of nice to take a moment and just... relax. Who knew petting puppies was so relaxing? Maybe more so for her than them. Her pulse slowed from its riotous pace from racing after the dogs. She took in a deep breath. Whatever happened would happen.

Since when had she gotten all zen?

She looked up when Ben walked back a few minutes later. "Gary is coming to get us to take you to the inn. Mom made it to the inn when she was searching for you on the beach, so he'll pick her up and take her back home to get ready and he'll drop off the pups. Sara is headed to go pick up your dress and bring it back to the inn."

"My things I need to get ready are in my car."

"Got it." Ben texted Sara. "There, she'll get your things, too."

He reached down and pulled her to her feet. "See, it's all going to be fine."

She looked down at the sand stuck to her legs and knew she needed another shower. Her hair tossed wildly around her face. It was going to take a miracle to get her ready on time.

Ben pulled her into his arms and kissed her. "It's really going to be okay. Honest."

CHAPTER 15

R obin, relief surging through her, hugged her friend as soon as Charlotte entered The Nest. "I'm so glad you're all right."

Charlotte looked at the clock on the wall. "I'm fine, but I now have one hour to get ready. And I need another shower."

Robin thrust a towel toward Charlotte. "Here, use the bathroom in the hallway. Take a quick, cool shower. We've got this."

Charlotte didn't look convinced but hurried down the hallway to the shower.

Five minutes later Charlotte walked into the bedroom, wrapped in the towel, her hair dripping. Robin pointed to a chair. "Sit, I'm going to blow dry your hair. Then I'll do your makeup. As soon as Sara gets back with your dress, you'll get dressed. Then I'll put your hair up. In the meantime... you drink some water." She thrust a glass of ice water at her friend.

By the time she'd dried Charlotte's hair and did her makeup, Sara returned with the dress. They helped her slip it on.

"Oh, Charlotte. You look beautiful." Robin had to chase tears from the corner of her eyes.

"You do, Char." Sara walked up beside her.

"Sit and let me do up your hair. See, I told you that you'd be ready in time. We have..." She glanced at the clock and laughed. "Minutes to spare."

"They won't start without the bride, anyway."

Robin twisted Charlotte's hair into a loose bun with tendrils curling around her face. It was the perfect look for Charlotte.

They headed out to the main room of The Nest. Someone knocked at the door and Sara answered it.

Eva and Charlotte's mother. Robin took a deep breath, wondering how this would turn out.

Mrs. Duncan entered the room and stared at her daughter. "Charlotte, you look lovely."

Robin had to keep her mouth from gaping open in surprise. *A compliment?*

Eva stood beside her mother. "That dress does... suit you," she said with reluctance evident in her voice.

Robin looked over at Sara and saw the stunned look on her face.

"I was wondering... and I should have asked you earlier. But would you like to wear the pearls I wore at my wedding? They were your father's mother's. She gave them to me on our wedding day." Mrs. Duncan held out a strand of pearls.

"Oh, Mom. I'd love to."

Mrs. Duncan came over and placed the necklace around Charlotte's neck and fastened it. "There, that looks perfect."

Charlotte glanced in the mirror, fingering the pearls. "It does look perfect. Thank you."

"They do look lovely." Robin smiled at her friend.

Charlotte turned back to her mother and sister. "Have you seen outside? Doesn't it look great?"

"There's just so much... red." Eva frowned slightly.

"Yes, there is a lot of it. It is a Christmas

wedding, you know." Charlotte smiled broadly at her sister.

"Oh, Charlotte, your shoes." Sara laughed and held out the red shoes. "You still need those."

"That's what you're wearing to the wedding? Red shoes? *Flats* at that?" Eva rolled her eyes. "It's your *wedding*. You're not even wearing heels?"

"Have you ever tried walking on sand in heels?" Charlotte rolled her eyes right back at Eva.

Good for Charlotte.

Eva continued. "And what's this about serving *cookies*? You can't serve cookies instead of a cake."

Robin swiveled her head to look at Charlotte to see how she was going to handle this. Should she step in and run interference? Charlotte didn't need this on her wedding day. Or ever, for that matter.

Charlotte looked at her sister for a moment before she answered. "And yet we are serving cookies. And I'm perfectly fine with it. Have you seen how Julie decorates Christmas cookies? They are like works of art." Charlotte turned her back on her sister and fingered the pearls again.

"Your whole wedding is turning into a disaster." Eva's voice was tinged with disapproval. No, more like *filled* with disapproval.

Charlotte spun back around and stood in front of her sister. Robin expected to see the face she made when she was counting to three—or ten. But no, Charlotte plunged right in.

"Eva, you're my sister. That's why you're invited. But I will not have you criticizing anything about my wedding. It's my special day. I'm happy with all my decisions and how everything turned out. I'm serious. No more. I'm finished listening to your remarks. Stay and enjoy yourself or go. At this point, I don't care. But you will not ruin this day for me.

"Well, I never," Eva sputtered, and her face turned crimson red.

At least Eva's face would go with the red Christmas decorations she detested so much...

Oops, that was an uncharitable thought.

"You're right. You never. You never think before you spout off your thoughts. And I frankly don't want to hear them today."

Robin stood back in amazement. She wanted to start a slow clap applause but figured that was out of line. She smothered a grin. And that alone was hard. Very hard.

Mrs. Duncan reached out a hand. "Eva, let's not upset Charlotte. It's her special day. I want it to be... perfect."

Robin almost broke into applause for Mrs. Duncan now.

"But, Mother—"

Mrs. Duncan held up a hand. "Come, it's almost time for the ceremony to start. Let's head out and let Charlotte do any last-minute primping she needs to do. You look lovely, dear. You're going to have a wonderful wedding." Mrs. Duncan walked over and kissed Charlotte's cheek. Char's eyes filled with tears.

"Thanks, Mom."

Mrs. Duncan and Eva left The Nest, and Charlotte turned to face Robin, her eyes glistening with unshed tears. "Who was that woman and what did she do with my mother?"

Robin laughed. "The new and improved Mrs. Duncan? She was... really sweet."

"She was." Charlotte nodded.

"And you stood up to Eva. You were magnificent." Sara hugged Charlotte.

"So, are you ready?" Robin asked.

"Never been more so. And thank you for helping me get ready. I can't believe we pulled this off in an hour."

"You do look beautiful." Robin kissed Charlotte's cheek. "Come on. You've got some aisle walking to do."

CHAPTER 16

Charlotte held onto her father's arm as she walked down the aisle toward Ben. If she didn't know better, she'd say there were tears threatening to spill on her almost-husband's face. He swore he never cried. And he looked impossibly handsome standing up by the arbor with Jay and David.

Her father paused at the end of the aisle and turned to her. "I love you, Charlotte. Much happiness to both of you." He kissed her as Ben stepped near and took her hand.

Her father went back to sit by her mother as she stood facing Ben, searching his face, and memorizing every detail of this wonderful moment.

Even though she was technically about fifteen minutes late, the sunset had cooperated with her delay. The sky began to erupt into brilliant shades of orange and pink, and a lovely warm light flowed around them.

Ben squeezed her hand, then leaned over and whispered, "You look beautiful."

She glanced over at Robin and Sara. Both of them were fighting back tears. Happy tears. Just like she had at their weddings, these friends she loved so much. She reached down and touched the side of her wedding dress, feeling the letter from Barbara in the hidden pocket with its message of love and good wishes.

She turned back to Ben, a beaming smile stretched across her face. His smile matched hers and he squeezed her hands.

The minister led them through their vows, and Ben held her hand tightly throughout the service until he slipped the simple wedding band on her finger and she gave Ben his ring.

Just as they were finishing, she looked up and the twinkle lights lit up all over the arbor. Before she could even comprehend it, it was over, and Ben leaned in to kiss her. Then he scooped her up in a hug, laughing, then set her down.

"Meet Mrs. Hallet. And I'm her very happy husband."

The guests rose to their feet, clapping. Ben took her hand and they walked back down the aisle together. Husband and wife. Married.

Happiness surged through her, and as much as she could tell, she did get her wish. Everything *was* perfect.

CHARLOTTE AND BEN circled around their family and friends at the wedding, making sure they spoke to everyone. Ben held her hand and kissed her often, a smile permanently etched across his handsome features. This wonderful husband of hers.

"We should go say something to Eva." She looked at Ben for support as she tugged the wrap Lillian had made close around her shoulders.

"We should. You ready for that?"

"Nothing she says can dampen my spirits. I feel on top of the world tonight."

He kissed her yet again and whispered, "I love to hear that."

They headed over to where Eva was standing

by the dessert table—with one of those frowned upon Christmas cookies in her hand—and she turned as they approached.

"There's the happy couple."

"Are you having a good time?" Ben asked politely.

"Yes, it's fine." Eva sighed. "Unconventional and *basic*, but I suppose it's what Charlotte wanted. She's always been a little... different. And you just had that tiny, simple cake to cut. Just... not what a wedding is supposed to be like."

"It's exactly what both Charlotte and I wanted," Ben asserted as he covered her hand resting on his arm.

"I would never have had a wedding as... *simple* as this. A wedding should be carefully planned and... well... special."

"Today was special, Eva. Very special. Perfect, even." She turned to Ben. "We should go and see Tally over there. It was so nice of her to come." She left her sister behind but didn't miss her taking another of the beautiful and delicious Christmas cookies.

Charlotte glanced one more time at Eva. Some things will never change. Her sister would never approve of what she did, or said, or wore.

But as she looked up into her husband's face, so full of love, she no longer cared what Eva thought or said. Truly.

They walked over to Tally and the woman hugged them both. "It was such a wonderful wedding, just perfect," Tally said.

See, there's another person who thought it was perfect.

"Thank you. I thought it was wonderful, too. And I'm so grateful that you had an opening for a wedding at Magic Cafe tonight so I could still have my wedding here at Charming Inn."

"I'm glad it worked out. I know how close you are to Lillian and Sara. And this place is..." Tally grinned. "Well... *charming*."

They all laughed.

She and Ben continued to visit with guests. At one point she glanced over and saw Eva deep in conversation with Camille Montgomery, frowns of disapproval etched on their faces. Ah, kindred spirits. Eva had probably found an ally in Camille. Camille was just as critical about everything as Eva.

But neither one of them could touch her tonight. Not after this wedding. Not with this wonderful man by her side.

She rose up on tiptoe and kissed his cheek. "You know, that legend is true."

"The one about wishes at Lighthouse Point? Of course, it's true." He smiled.

"And my wish came true. Everything was perfect."

"And my wish came true."

"You made a wish?"

"I did. I wished for you. And look at this? We're married." He kissed her gently. "Those wishes made at Lighthouse Point are powerful things."

And he was right. The wishes were powerful desires their hearts put out to the universe.

And she had everything her heart desired right here. Ben, her friends, the island.

"I love you," she whispered to her husband.

"And I love you, Mrs. Hallet." And he kissed her again. And once more for good measure.

CHAPTER 17

Charlotte and Ben had the perfect honeymoon aboard Lady Belle. She was so surprised at how Ben had decorated the boat with Christmas decorations and flowers. It looked magical. And he'd planned delicious food for all their meals. They spent hours just sitting on deck talking in the sunshine and sipping champagne at night with only the stars and moonlight illuminating the deck. It was the definition of romantic as far as she was concerned. And if it were possible, she fell even more in love with the man she'd married.

At the end of the honeymoon, they reluctantly returned to Belle Island. The evening was approaching as they docked the boat and climbed off. She hated for the honeymoon to end, but she was excited to get to their new home. They drove from the marina to their new house.

She gasped when they pulled up. "Oh, Ben. Look. It's all decorated for Christmas."

"Really?" His face held a wide grin. "Hm. Imagine that."

White Christmas lights twinkled across their front porch. A wreath with a pretty red bow hung on their door. Greenery twined around the porch posts. "How did this happen?"

"Might have had a bit of help from Robin and Sara. They planned it all and decorated while we were gone."

"Oh, Ben. It's wonderful." She hugged him tightly.

They got out of the car, and as they got to the front door Ben turned to her. "Wait." He unlocked the door, turned back to her, and scooped her up in his arms. "I've got to carry you over the threshold."

She laughed in delight at his gesture.

He carried her inside, kissed her, and set her down. She turned and gasped with pleasure. "Look, a Christmas tree. And more decorations"

She walked over to the tree and looked at the

cutout ornaments hanging on the tree. She turned one over, then the next, tears pricking the corners of her eyes.

"Oh, look, Ben. These are all well wishes from the guests at our wedding. It's all so—"

"Perfect?" Ben grinned.

"Yes, exactly." She smiled back and walked into his embrace.

CHRISTMAS EVE

O n Christmas Eve Charlotte stood with her friends on the deck at Magic Cafe. Tally had closed the restaurant to the public for the evening and invited close friends for a Christmas Eve party. The weather had cooperated with a delightful evening, not too chilly, and a brilliant sunset was beginning to unfurl overhead.

Ben stood chatting with Jay and glanced over and smiled at her. She smiled back as contentment washed through her.

She glanced over at where Tally stood with Julie and Susan from Belle Island Inn. The three of them were best friends, just like she was with Robin and Sara.

Ruby and Lillian stood a short distance away chatting with Dorothy and some of their Yarnie friends. This island made for some of the most enduring friendships ever. It was part of the magic of the island.

She smiled at all the people here who she loved so much. All the wonderful people from their town.

Friendships ran deep between the women on Belle Island, and her friendship with Robin and Sara was unbreakable. Gratitude and love flowed through her.

She turned back to her friends. "Do you remember the summer after we graduated from high school? We went to Lighthouse Point?"

"I remember." Sara smiled. "We all made the same wish and tossed in our shells."

"That even though we were all headed in different directions, we wished that we'd always stay best friends." Robin's mouth tilted in a smile.

"And we did stay best of friends, didn't we?" She put an arm around each of them.

"And we always will," Robin added.

She took her arms from around her friends and whirled to face them, grinning. "Race you to the water's edge."

Robin laughed and kicked off her shoes. "I'm going to win."

"No, you're not," Sara said as she kicked off her shoes and sprinted toward the sand.

Charlotte let out a delighted peal of laughter and chased after her friends.

With that, the three friends laughed and raced toward the sea. Best friends.

Forever.

Just like all the friendships built and love found at Lighthouse Point.

DEAR READER,

I hope you enjoyed this short holiday read as I wrapped up the Charming Inn series. (Though, I never say never on adding to a series at some future point!). It you enjoyed this series, have you read the Lighthouse Point series? Try Wish Upon a Shell - Book One in that series.

And look for the Moonbeam Bay series, releasing in January 2021!

While you wait, have you read the Sweet River series? It's the perfect series to binge-read!

See all my books at kaycorrell.com/books.

As always, thanks for reading my stories. I truly appreciate all my readers.

Happy reading,

Kay

ALSO BY KAY CORRELL

COMFORT CROSSING ~ THE SERIES

The Shop on Main - Book One

The Memory Box - Book Two

The Christmas Cottage - A Holiday Novella
(Book 2.5)

The Letter - Book Three

The Christmas Scarf - A Holiday Novella (Book 3.5)

The Magnolia Cafe - Book Four

The Unexpected Wedding - Book Five

The Wedding in the Grove (crossover short story
between series - Josephine and Paul from The Letter.)

LIGHTHOUSE POINT ~ THE SERIES

Wish Upon a Shell - Book One

Wedding on the Beach - Book Two

Love at the Lighthouse - Book Three

Cottage near the Point - Book Four

Return to the Island - Book Five

Bungalow by the Bay - Book Six

CHARMING INN ~ Return to Lighthouse Point

One Simple Wish - Book One

Two of a Kind - Book Two

Three Little Things - Book Three

Four Short Weeks - Book Four

Five Years or So - Book Five

Six Hours Away - Book Six

Charming Christmas - Book Seven

SWEET RIVER ~ THE SERIES

A Dream to Believe in - Book One

A Memory to Cherish - Book Two

A Song to Remember - Book Three

A Time to Forgive - Book Four

A Summer of Secrets - Book Five

A Moment in the Moonlight - Book Six

MOONBEAM BAY - coming 2021

The Parker Women

The Parker Cafe

A Heather Parker Original

The Parker Family Secret

Grace Parker's Peach Pie

INDIGO BAY ~ Save by getting Kay's complete collection of stories previously published separately in the multi-author Indigo Bay series. The three stories are all interconnected.

Sweet Days by the Bay

Or buy them separately:

Sweet Sunrise - Book Three

Sweet Holiday Memories - A short holiday story

Sweet Starlight - Book Nine

ABOUT THE AUTHOR

Kay writes sweet, heartwarming stories that are a cross between women's fiction and contemporary romance. She is known for her charming small towns, quirky townsfolk, and enduring strong friendships between the women in her books.

Kay lives in the Midwest of the U.S. and can often be found out and about with her camera, taking a myriad of photographs which she likes to incorporate into her book covers. When not lost in her writing or photography, she can be found spending time with her ever-supportive husband, knitting, or playing with her puppies—two cavaliers and one naughty but adorable Australian shepherd. Kay and her husband also love to travel. When it comes to vacation time, she is torn between a nice trip to the beach or the mountains —but the mountains only get considered in the summer—she swears she's allergic to snow.

Learn more about Kay and her books at
kaycorrell.com

While you're there, sign up for her newsletter to
hear about new releases, sales, and giveaways.

WHERE TO FIND ME:
kaycorrell.com
authorcontact@kaycorrell.com

Join my Facebook Reader Group. We have lots of
fun and you'll hear about sales and new releases
first!
https://www.facebook.com/groups/KayCorrell/

I love to hear from my readers. Feel free to
contact me at authorcontact@kaycorrell.com

facebook.com/KayCorrellAuthor
instagram.com/kaycorrell
pinterest.com/kaycorrellauthor
amazon.com/author/kaycorrell
bookbub.com/authors/kay-correll